Date: 01/23/12

Revised and Updated

War Planes

Tactical Fighters
The F-15 Eagles

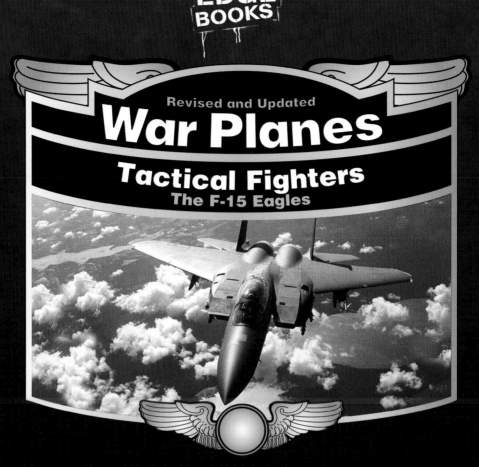

by Michael and Gladys Green

Consultant:
Raymond L. Puffer, PhD, Historian
Air Force Flight Test Center
Edwards Air Force Base, California

Capstone
press®

Mankato, Minnesota

Edge Books are published by Capstone Press,
151 Good Counsel Drive, P.O. Box 669, Mankato, Minnesota 56002.
www.capstonepress.com

Library of Congress Cataloging-in-Publication Data
Green, Michael, 1952–
    Tactical fighters : the F-15 eagles / by Michael and Gladys Green — Rev.
and updated.
        p. cm. — (Edge books. War planes)
        Includes bibliographical references and index.
        ISBN-13: 978-1-4296-1321-7 (hardcover)
        ISBN-10: 1-4296-1321-1 (hardcover)
        1. Eagle (Jet fighter plane) — Juvenile literature. I. Green, Gladys, 1954– II. Title.
III. Series.
UG1242.F5G715 2008
623.74'64 — dc22   2007031337

Summary: Introduces the F-15 Eagles, their specifications, weapons, missions, and
    future in the Air Force.

Editorial Credits

Carrie A. Braulick, editor; Jo Miller, photo researcher; Katy Kudela, revised
    edition editor; Kyle Grenz, revised edition designer

Photo Credits

Boeing Management Company, 13
Defense Visual Information Center (DVIC), 1, 4, 7, 9, 16–17, 18, 20,
    23, 26, 29; MSGT Marvin Krause, cover
Photo by Ted Carlson/Fotodynamics, 10, 24

1 2 3 4 5 6 13 12 11 10 09 08

Table of Contents

Chapter 1

The F-15 in Action

Learn about
- The F-15's mission
- F-15 design
- F-15 models

Late one night, four U.S. Air Force pilots are flying F-15 Eagle fighter planes over a friendly country. A radio message tells them 10 enemy planes are approaching.

The F-15 pilots turn their aircraft toward the enemy planes. A powerful radar in each F-15's nose locates the other planes about 100 miles (160 kilometers) away. The enemy pilots fire missiles at the F-15s. The F-15 pilots turn sharply and dive at high speeds to avoid the missiles. They then fire their own missiles at the enemy planes. Four of the enemy fighters explode.

The F-15 pilots fire more missiles. Another four enemy planes explode. The last two enemy pilots turn around and try to fly away. The F-15 pilots catch up to them and use their planes' M61A1 Vulcan cannons to shoot down the enemy planes.

Building the F-15

In the early 1960s, the Air Force wanted fast planes that could easily defeat enemy planes. The Air Force wanted to replace its F-4 Phantom IIs with improved fighters.

In 1972, aircraft manufacturer McDonnell Douglas produced a test model of a one-seat fighter called the F-15A. In 1974, the Air Force began to fly final models of the F-15A and F-15B. The F-15B is a two-seat training version of the F-15A.

McDonnell Douglas continued to build other F-15 models for the Air Force. In 1979, the improved F-15C one-seat model entered Air Force service. Later that year, Air Force pilots began to fly a two-seat training version of the F-15C called the F-15D.

The F-15E is designed to attack ground targets.

The F-15E Strike Eagle is the newest F-15
model. It entered Air Force service in 1988.
Today, the Air Force flies more than 200
F-15Es. The two-seat F-15E has a different
mission from other F-15s. The F-15E is both
a ground-attack plane and a fighter plane.
After it drops bombs on an enemy target,
it can fight enemy planes in the air.

The Boeing Company bought McDonnell Douglas Corporation in 1997. Boeing then continued to build F-15Es for the Air Force.

About the F-15

The F-15 is one of the world's most advanced fighter planes. It has a perfect combat record. No enemy forces have shot down an F-15 during combat.

Today, the Air Force has more than 700 F-15s. Air Force pilots fly the F-15C, the F-15D, and the F-15E Strike Eagle. Air National Guard units use the F-15A and the F-15B to support the Air Force.

EDGE FACT

The Air Force gives each type of aircraft a nickname. The F-15 pilots call their jets "Eagles" out of pride.

Inside the F-15

Learn about

- F-15 engines
- F-15 controls
- LANTIRN system

The F-15 is a large aircraft compared to other modern fighters. It is more than 63 feet (19 meters) long. The distance between its wings is almost 43 feet (13 meters). The F-15 has a broad back between its wings. This design helps F-15s take off fast and turn easily in the air.

The F-15's size gives its pilots advantages. The F-15 flies farther and faster than smaller fighters. It also carries more weapons than smaller fighter planes.

Powerful Engines

Two large jet engines power each F-15. Each F-15C and F-15D engine produces almost 23,450 pounds (10,637 kilograms) of thrust to push the aircraft through the air. Each F-15E engine produces 29,000 pounds (13,154 kilograms) of thrust.

The F-15 is one of the fastest fighters in the world. Its engines give it a top speed of 1,875 miles (3,017 kilometers) per hour. But pilots usually fly the F-15 at high speeds only when flying into or out of battle areas. Fighter pilots often need to turn sharply. A fighter flying at top speed cannot turn without slowing down. F-15 pilots usually fly at speeds of less than 600 miles (966 kilometers) per hour.

EDGE FACT

An Air Force ground crew can replace the engine of an F-15 Eagle in less than an hour.

The F-15's cockpit has a control stick and a throttle.

Inside the Cockpit

The pilot sits in a cockpit in the front of the plane. A pilot's main controls are the control stick and the throttle. Pilots use the control stick to steer their planes. Pilots control the speed of their aircraft with the throttle. Pilots also can use controls on the throttle to release missiles.

All F-15s have a screen called a head-up display (HUD). The HUD allows pilots to view flight information without looking down at cockpit controls.

F-15E LANTIRN System

The F-15E has a LANTIRN (Low Altitude Navigation Targeting Infrared for Night) system to help pilots perform missions at night and during bad weather conditions. The LANTIRN system is located under the aircraft's body in **pods**.

One pod contains navigational equipment. This equipment helps the F-15E's crew keep track of the plane's surroundings. The equipment includes a terrain-following radar (TFR) and a Forward-Looking Infrared (FLIR) sensor. The TFR allows pilots to see objects in their flight path on a screen. The FLIR sensor detects heat given off by objects. Information from the FLIR sensor appears on the pilot's HUD.

pod — a storage area under the wings or body of an aircraft

Function:	Air-to-ground attack aircraft
Manufacturer:	Boeing
Deployed:	1988
Length:	63 feet, 8 inches (19.4 meters)
Wingspan:	42 feet, 8 inches (13 meters)
Height:	18 feet, 5 inches (5.6 meters)
Weight:	81,000 pounds (36,700 kilograms)
Payload:	24,000 pounds (10,886 kilograms)
Engine:	Two Pratt & Whitney F100-PW-220 or 229 turbofans
Speed:	1,875 miles (3,017 kilometers) per hour
Range:	2,400 miles (3,862 kilometers); unlimited with in-flight refueling

The second pod contains devices to help the F-15E's crew hit targets. A tracking FLIR sensor allows the crew to see targets on a screen. It can show targets that are up to 10 miles (16 kilometers) away.

nose

fuel tank

The F-15 Eagle

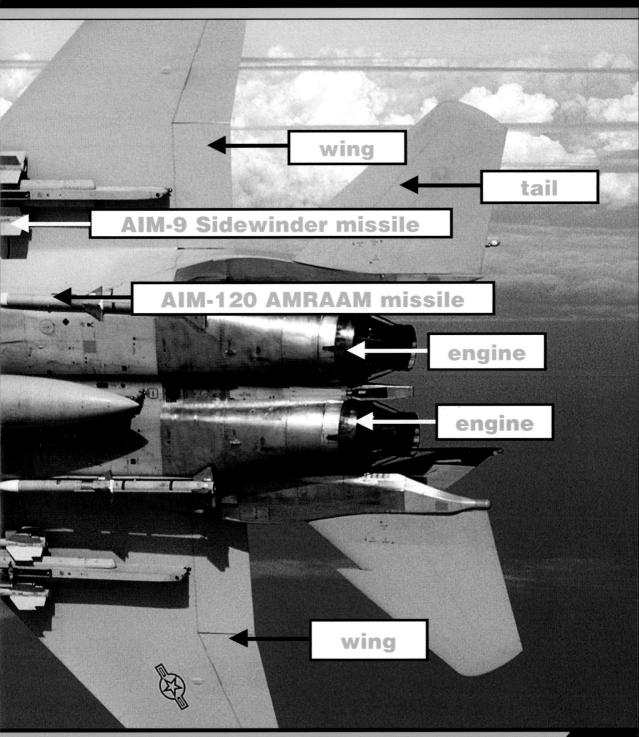

wing

tail

AIM-9 Sidewinder missile

AIM-120 AMRAAM missile

engine

engine

wing

Weapons and Tactics

Learn about
- F-15 missiles
- Laser-guided bombs
- Protection systems

F-15s can carry equipment and weapons that weigh nearly 24,000 pounds (10,886 kilograms). All models can carry a M61A1 Vulcan and eight air-to-air missiles.

The F-15E usually carries bombs and air-to-ground missiles instead of air-to-air missiles. The F-15E has a Weapon System Operator (WSO). This crewmember releases the F-15E's ground attack weapons and runs the plane's radar unit and protection systems.

The AIM-9 Sidewinder is a heat-seeking missile.

Automatic Cannon

The F-15's M61A1 Vulcan cannon is located in its right wing. The Vulcan holds shells called rounds. It can fire more than 6,000 rounds in one minute. It has a range of about .5 mile (.8 kilometer).

Air-to-Air Missiles

The F-15 carries air-to-air missiles under its body and wings. The missiles can be heat-seeking or radar-guided missiles.

A heat-seeking missile has a sensor in its nose. The sensor guides the missile toward the heat from an enemy plane's exhaust. The F-15's heat-seeking missile is called the AIM-9 Sidewinder. It has a range of about 10 miles (16 kilometers).

F-15 pilots aim a radar beam at a target to fire radar-guided missiles. The missiles then follow the beam to the target. F-15 pilots often use the AIM-7 Sparrow missile at night and during bad weather conditions. The AIM-7 has a 90-pound (41-kilogram) explosive called a warhead in its nose. It has a range of about 30 miles (48 kilometers).

F-15 pilots use the radar-guided AIM-120 Advanced Medium-Range Air-to-Air Missile (AMRAAM) for targets that are farther away. This missile has a range of almost 40 miles (64 kilometers).

F-15E Bombs

The F-15E can carry almost any of the Air Force's air-to-ground weapons. These weapons include unguided bombs and laser-guided bombs (LGBs). Unguided bombs fall to the ground freely. **Laser beams** guide LGBs to targets. An F-15E's WSO or a crewmember from another plane aims a laser beam at a target. The LGB has a sensor that detects the beam of light.

The GBU-28 is one of the most powerful LGBs that the F-15E carries. The Air Force calls the GBU-28 the "Bunker Buster." It is designed to blow up underground enemy hideouts called bunkers. The GBU-28 weighs about 5,000 pounds (2,300 kilograms) and is almost 20 feet (6 meters) long.

F-15E Missiles

The F-15E can carry air-to-ground missiles. The AGM-65G Maverick has a 300-pound (136-kilogram) warhead. It can hit targets more than 10 miles (16 kilometers) away.

F-15Es sometimes carry Mark 84 LGBs.

WSOs can use the AGM-130 air-to-ground missile to hit long-range targets. The AGM-130 has a range of 40 miles (64 kilometers) and has a 2,000-pound (907-kilogram) warhead.

laser beam — a narrow, intense beam of light

Combat Tactics

The F-15 has features that help pilots control it during combat. It has low wing loading. The aircraft's weight is low compared to the size of its wings. The F-15 also has a great deal of thrust compared to its weight. These features help pilots make sharp turns at high speeds.

F-15 pilots need to know when enemy weapons approach their aircraft. The F-15 has a radar warning system. The system detects radar signals and shows their most likely source. Pilots can see this information on a cockpit screen.

The F-15E's WSO can try to protect the plane after receiving information from the radar warning system. The WSO may release small pieces of **chaff**. Each piece of chaff reflects radar energy to the enemy radar station. The enemy radar then does not work properly. The WSO also can use the F-15E's radar jammer. The jammer sends out powerful electronic signals that stop enemy radar from working properly.

chaff — strips of metal foil dropped by an aircraft to confuse enemy radar

Serving the Military

Learn about

- F-15 improvements
- F-22A Raptor
- Future of Air Force fighters

The F-15 has been one of the Air Force's most important fighters for more than 25 years. Throughout the years, the Air Force has updated much of the aircraft's equipment. Improvements make the plane's systems and weapons even more useful.

JDAMs

In 2003, the F-15E began carrying a type of smart bomb called the Joint Direct Attack Munition (JDAM). The JDAM includes a kit that fits over the tail of an unguided bomb to turn it into a guided bomb.

Spacecraft called satellites guide JDAMs. Poor weather conditions can cause LGBs to stray from their flight path. Weather conditions do not affect satellite-guided weapons.

The F-22A Raptor

Even with improvements, older F-15 models are wearing out. In the 1970s, the Air Force began planning to replace the F-15C. After testing experimental models, the Air Force chose the F-22A Raptor as the replacement plane. A two-seat version of the F-22A called the F-22B will replace the F-15D. The F-15E will remain in Air Force service until about 2030.

EDGE FACT

Israel, Saudi Arabia, and Japan each use a model of the F-15 in their air forces.

The F-22A Raptor is a replacement plane for the F-15C.

The F-22A is the world's most advanced fighter plane. It uses less fuel at high speeds than the F-15 does. The F-22A can fly 1,500 miles (2,400 kilometers) per hour for long periods of time.

Lockheed Martin and Boeing produce the F-22A. In the late 1990s, the Air Force flew test models of the fighter. In 2005, Air Force pilots began flying the F-22A. The F-22A represents the future of the Air Force.

GLOSSARY

chaff (CHAF) — strips of metal foil dropped by an aircraft to confuse enemy radar

laser beam (LAY-zur BEEM) — a narrow, intense beam of light

pod (POD) — a storage area under the wings or body of an aircraft

radar (RAY-dar) — equipment that uses radio waves to locate and guide objects

sensor (SEN-sur) — an instrument that detects physical changes in the environment

throttle (THROT-uhl) — a control on an airplane that allows pilots to increase or decrease the plane's speed

thrust (THRUHST) — the force created by a jet engine; thrust pushes an airplane forward.

warhead (WOR-hed)—the explosive part of a missile or rocket

READ MORE

Abramson, Andra Serlin. *Fighter Planes Up Close.* New York: Sterling, 2008.

Doeden, Matt. *The U.S. Air Force.* The U.S. Armed Forces. Mankato, Minn.: Capstone Press, 2005.

Zuehlke, Jeffrey. *Fighter Planes.* Pull Ahead Books. Minneapolis: Lerner, 2006.

INTERNET SITES

FactHound offers a safe, fun way to find Internet sites related to this book. All of the sites on FactHound have been researched by our staff.

Here's how:
1. Visit *www.facthound.com*
2. Choose your grade level.
3. Type in this book ID **1429613211** for age-appropriate sites. You may also browse subjects by clicking on letters, or by clicking on pictures and words.
4. Click on the **Fetch It** button.

FactHound will fetch the best sites for you!

INDEX